Daijha Road

C. Angel

WESTBOW
PRESS
A DIVISION OF THOMAS NELSON
& ZONDERVAN

Scripture taken from the King James Version of the Bible.

Scripture taken from the Holy Bible, NEW INTERNATIONAL VERSION®.
Copyright © 1973, 1978, 1984 by Biblica, Inc. All rights reserved worldwide.
Used by permission. NEW INTERNATIONAL VERSION® and NIV® are
registered trademarks of Biblica, Inc. Use of either trademark for the offering
of goods or services requires the prior written consent of Biblica US, Inc.

WestBow Press books may be ordered through booksellers or by contacting:

WestBow Press
A Division of Thomas Nelson & Zondervan
1663 Liberty Drive
Bloomington, IN 47403
www.westbowpress.com
1 (866) 928-1240

Because of the dynamic nature of the Internet, any web addresses or
links contained in this book may have changed since publication and
may no longer be valid. The views expressed in this work are solely those
of the author and do not necessarily reflect the views of the publisher,
and the publisher hereby disclaims any responsibility for them.

Any people depicted in stock imagery provided by Thinkstock are
models, and such images are being used for illustrative purposes only.
Certain stock imagery © Thinkstock.

ISBN: 978-1-4908-5203-4 (sc)
ISBN: 978-1-4908-5204-1 (hc)
ISBN: 978-1-4908-5202-7 (e)

Library of Congress Control Number: 2014916320

Printed in the United States of America.

WestBow Press rev. date: 10/31/2014

This book is dedicated to my Lord and Savior, Jesus Christ, God the Father, and the Holy Spirit. To my babies, Ce, Terrell II, and Hollis, God has used you three to help give my life meaning and purpose. I'm praying I can do right by Him, you, and your dad in raising you to be the best you can possibly be. Love you to life! Christina—what can I say? Our friendship has spanned our lives. You are a soul tie I thank God for all the time. Love ya dearest! Jade, Sha'Rona, and Kim (my girls!), I prayed for God to raise me up some godly female friends when I moved—He surpassed my expectations with you three. Girls' nights (and all our times in between) are *awesome*. I love you guys! Jonnetta, cuz, I thank God for you. Our friendship has grown and matured. Thank you for introducing me to Mr. Burton! Traci, Carmen, and Adam—my sisters and bro, my fam!—I have *so* many stories to tell, but I'll just say this: thanks for having my back, fighting for me, dragging me over the tracks, and snatching up every stray hair on my head to keep me looking presentable! I love you guys forever and always! Mom and dad, I thank you always—love you forever. To my church family: I didn't understand the meaning of "church family" until I was blessed with you wonderful people at New Antioch Bible Fellowship (NABF). You've seen me through so much, supported me through more, and continue to be my safe place. NABF is the "Best branch of Zion this side of the Jordan!" Pastor Hayes and Sister Mary, you two are godsends. I love you and we thank you. And to the late Terrell Burton Sr., thank you for three of the best blessings of my life. To all my family and friends who have touched my life, thank you, and I love you all.

"For I know the plans that I have for you," declares
the Lord, *"plans to prosper you and not to harm
you, plans to give you hope and a future."*[1]
Jeremiah 29:11 (New International Version)

1   New International Version. [Colorado Springs]: Biblica, 2011.
    BibleGateway.com. Web. 3 Mar. 2011.

Home is less than great. Junior high school is awful. Daijha's mom is rarely around, but when she is, there is turmoil. This leaves Daijha alone and afraid. School should be an escape from her loneliness, but instead, it is a daily torment Daijha endures that further isolates her.

Things begin to change when J enrolls in school. She has sass and confidence—and a whole bunch of extra weight! How can she be so confident looking the way that she does? Is it real, or is she faking? Where does it come from?

J is not at all intimidated and has an inner strength Daijha knows not of. She stands up for herself and shows Daijha a thing or two in the process.

Chapter 1

"Nee, come on!"

My sister is impatiently hollering her nickname for me from downstairs. My name is actually Daijha. Daijha LeNeece Compton. My first name is pronounced Daze-ja, but she calls me Nee, from my middle name. I run down a few stairs and peek around the corner. She is standing by the door, looking out of place in the shabby living room. It was once her home too, but she moved out two years ago. Oh, how I envy her!

"Give me just a couple more minutes. I'm getting my shoes on."

"Well, hurry up, Daijha!" She glances up the stairs and jingles her keys. "I'll be in the car." I run back up the stairs and look in disgust at my "shoes." Of course they aren't the latest, hot style that everyone is wearing. They look like them, sure, but they aren't them.

At one time, they were a gleaming white, and I was so proud and happy. They looked good then, with their gray and yellow trim, just like the newest hot style. But as I wore them, they got dirty fast and started to crack and bend in unnatural places, just like all cheap gym shoes. It's bad enough that I only have four pairs of pants that don't even fit right. They usually look terrible when I wear them with the few dingy, raggedy shirts I do have, but the sorry shoes— man, they are the worst. Everyone knows shoes make the outfit! Even if the outfit is a little worn, rockin' a hot, clean pair of shoes makes all the difference! Not having the right look really says a lot about you at Ethel C. Mariam Junior High. And none of it do you want to hear.

"Man, I need some new shoes," I mumble to myself. "Shoot, I need some new everything. I can't wait to get up out of here!" I snatch on my knock-offs and run down the stairs. I slam the door behind me and jump down the four stairs at the front of the house. I trot over to the car and climb in. My sister, Reeni, is waiting behind the wheel. As I shut the car door, Reeni closes her phone.

Renni turns and gives me a big ol' smile. "You ready to go?"

"Yes!" I lean back in the seat and feel myself relax for the first time in a long time, and I smile. I look over at my sister in appreciation—she is so beautiful!

At twenty-two, she is eight years older than I am. And at 5'11", she is also about eight inches taller. To me, she looks like an African queen with chocolate-brown skin. Reeni wears her hair in nice, neat locks that reach her shoulders. The tips are dyed an orange-red color. Today, she has them piled on top of her head, spilling out of an orange print scarf that matches her sleeveless orange capri set and orange sandals. She has big wooden print bangles on her arms and matching hoops in her ears. She doesn't even need makeup, but she wears a lip gloss and a light dusting of eye shadow.

As she pulls away from the curb, I look down at my faded and worn grey cargo pants, dingy, white T-shirt, and knock-off gym shoes. I know most people aren't usually able to tell what I'm thinking, but Reeni—she knows me better than anybody.

"What's up, Nee? Whatcha thinkin' 'bout?" She gives me a quick glance and returns her eyes to the road as she turns left onto Stenson.

I turn my head and gaze out the window.

"Nee?"

"Yeah?"

"What's the matter?"

I shrug my shoulders. "I'm good."

"No you're not, babe. Don't forget—I know you. You know I used to change your nasty butt, right?"

"Shut up!" I can't help it, I crack a small smile.

"It was nasty, too!" She scrunches up her nose and continues, "And stank-ay! You used to—"

"Okay! Okay!" I laugh and hold up my hands in surrender.

"What? I was just getting started! You don't want to hear anymore Little Nee stories? You used to love them."

"Yeah, that was when they were a lot less embarrassing!"

"Ooh. Well, tell ya what. You spill the beans about what's up, or I keep telling stories. And they can get a lot worse!" She looks at me menacingly and wiggles her eyebrows. "Like the time when you were four and you used to—"

"All right!" I holler, holding my hands over my ears and laughing. "Man, Reeni, I wish I could live with you. I hate it here." I stop smiling and laughing.

"Nee," Reeni softly starts.

"I know. I know. You don't have to say it." I cross my arms and glare out the window. I'm not even mad at my sister. She has her hands full with my nephew and niece. Anthony is six and Michelle is four. She is in school full-time to become a middle school teacher and works full-time at a correctional facility. She doesn't have much free time like she used to. I am just mad at my life.

"Where are Ant and Chelle?"

"With their dad. It's just me and you today!" She elbows me in the side.

"Cool."

As Reeni turns onto the highway, she asks, "Where's Mom?"

I shrug my shoulders. "I don't even know."

"She's probably out with her friends from work."

"Yeah. Whatever."

"Don't be like that, Nee. She tries."

"Whatever, Reeni. She used to try, when you and Maurice where younger, but with me ... it's all about her and what she wants. We barely have food. And look at my clothes!" I open my arms and look down at my clothes. "I ask her to just get me a few things, and she just yells and hollers and says she doesn't have any money. Then, she tops it all off with telling me about how raggedy my daddy is, and why don't I just ask him?"

I cross my arms again and sigh. "I'm just tired of it. She looks nice every day for work. Even when she comes home and changes out of her work clothes, she still looks nice. All I'm saying is, why can't I just get a few things for school?! I hate her!" I yell. Tears start to well up in my eyes. I wipe vigorously as they start to fall down my face. I hate to cry!

"Whoa, Daijha, whoa!" Reeni puts one hand up. "Now that's too much. You don't hate her, and you need to calm down a little." She opens the arm console between us, reaches in, and grabs some tissues. She hands them over to me.

"Man, whatever!" I take the tissue, wipe my eyes, cross my arms over my chest, and glare at her. "You don't have to deal with kids calling you names, telling you that you stink, and laughing and pointing at you. You don't have to—"

"But I did," Reeni cuts me off. "And I dealt with it, and so will you. I know you're mad, but you can either spend all your time mad at Mom, or you can spend it moving forward."

Reeni always says something like this when she talks about life with Janet, our mother. She knows just the right words to say to calm me down and get me to think about the big picture. She pulls into the parking lot of Top Mart, the lowest-priced department store that sells everything from food to clothing. She drives up and down the aisles trying to get a close space. She finally whips her silver Ford Taurus into a parking space a short distance from the door and turns toward me.

"Nee, I know it is hard for you right now. I was ready to leave, and I hate that I had to leave you, but I had to. I had Ant too early, and then Chelle ..." She looks into the distance for a moment and then turns back toward me. "I needed to get my education so I could provide for them. I don't want them to go through what I went through and what you're going through now. I had to move out and start to get my own." She places her hand on my shoulder. "You have just a few more years here, girl. Just a few more—then you're off to college, too!" She smiles real big, and so do I. "But in the meantime, the in-between time—let's go on a little shopping spree! I know your birthday is coming up, and I figured I could get you a few things. How about it?!"

I cannot believe it! I am going to get some new clothes! "For real, Reeni? For real?"

"Yeah, for real, Nee. Come on." She opens her car door and climbs out.

I jump out the car smiling so wide my jaw hurts. Reeni comes around the side of the car and slings her arm over my shoulder, and we walk into the building. Together. Just like old times.

*****

Reeni and I carry the bags up to the house. After we left Top Mart, we stopped and ate at a buffet where you chose your own meat and sides and they cook it in front of you. It was so delicious! So I was full and happy. I run the bags up to my room while Reeni waits downstairs. As I walk back down the stairs, she asks, "Mom's not here, is she? I just called her phone, and she didn't answer."

"Nah. She may not have minutes. But I looked upstairs and didn't see her. She's probably over her man's house."

"Her man's house? What do you mean by that?" Reeni looks at me questioningly. It has just been mom and me in the house for the last couple years, though I am the one who spends the most time here. Mom always has somewhere to be—and usually with some man. The current is James. He is cool and all, but he is old as heck! His skin is all wrinkly and brown. He looks like a wet paper bag! Yuck. He claims he's fifty-five, but I'm betting it's more like 105. But to me, either way, he's still too old to be with ma, who's only forty-five. When I commented on how old he looks, Mom got mad. She said it was grown folks' business and to stay out of it. Looking at Reeni now, I know she doesn't really know too much about what is going on, and I don't want her to worry about taking care of me. I can take care of myself. So since I already decided I wasn't going to worry her, I lie.

"I'm jus' playing, Reeni. I don't even know if she has a man."

Reeni looks at me like she knows good and well I'm lying, but I guess she decides to play along, because she stops with the questions. Instead, she glances at her watch and says, "Well, I'll wait here 'til mom gets home."

I know Reeni has a lot to do and needs to be going soon. She lives two hours away and isn't able to come home to visit all the time. When the kids are with their dad, she packs in all her visits to her old friends and some family. It is cool that she stopped in with me for a while. It makes me feel special. However, I know she needs to go, but she is worried about me.

"Reeni, you don't have to stay. My dad will be by in a little while," I say. I don't truly know if he is coming or not, but I'll call him when she leaves.

Reeni looks torn. "You sure, Nee?"

I laugh. "Yeah, I'm a big girl. I'll be all right!"

"Okay, Nee." She bends forward and gives me a hug. "I'll call you later and make sure you are okay. Love ya!"

After Reeni leaves, I call my dad's house. He doesn't answer. He doesn't carry a cell phone—says it is too much money. I think for a minute and remember he has to work tonight.

"Well," I say to myself, "I guess it's just me tonight." I make sure the doors and windows are locked and all the lights are on, and then I race up the stairs. I hate being home alone, especially at night. I hate the dark! The house is big and creepy and has too many doors. I know monsters aren't real, per se. But my imagination is so vivid, I picture all types of crazy semihuman beings crawling out from under beds, busting through windows—just out to get me in general. This is why I cannot watch scary movies. I just know the events in the movie will happen to me, somehow. I feel safer when other people are around, so I usually just sit outside until it gets dark, but it is already beginning to get dark. No use sitting outside for five minutes.

When I get to my room, I shut the door and push my bed in front of it. I check under my bed after I move it, check the closet, and make sure the window is shut tight. Once I feel safe, I sit down on the bed. I look over at the stuff my sister bought for me and smile. I grab the bags and pull out three new pairs of jeans, an orange T-shirt with a music note on the front, a red-and-pink-striped polo shirt, and a blue shirt that is light at the top and gradually becomes darker toward the bottom. I also have a new pair of dark blue canvas high-tops. They didn't have any particular name, but I am happy. Monday will be a good day.

I strip out of my clothes and pull on some old shorts and a T-shirt. I pull my covers back and climb into bed. I grab my book out from under my pillow and begin to read. After about an hour, Mom still isn't home, and I put the book down on the floor and cover my whole body, head and all, with the blankets. I quietly listen to the house creak and try not to be too scared as I doze off.

*****

Mom comes home Saturday afternoon while my dad and I are sitting on the porch laughing. He called and checked on me last night and again this morning. He only works a few minutes away from Mom's house, and he once told me that he drives by at night, on his lunch break, and checks the doors.

This makes me feel a little safer. We both look out to the curb as Mom pulls up. She gets out of the car, walks around it, comes up the steps, and says hi without even looking at us before walking into the house.

I turn to my father. "Can I please come live with you, Dad?"

"Dai, you know you can't. I don't have enough room."

"Come on, Dad!" I start to beg. "Please? I'll sleep on the couch—I don't care!"

Dad sighs. "I know you will." Dad hates this conversation, and I know it. We have it often, but I can't help but have it. Sometimes, I don't think the problem is so much about room. I think that he kind of enjoys living alone, but I am tired of living with Mom. She doesn't care about me, and I am tired of staying here! Who just walks by their child without so much as a glance?! At least with my dad, I eat regularly, even if it is chicken most nights.

But when I really think about it, my dad's house isn't anywhere I really want to be, either. My dad isn't the cleanest person in the world, and his house shows that. There are often clothes lying around and dirty dishes all over kitchen. The carpet is dirty and the furniture shabby. But the difference is that, at my dad's, he and I talk and laugh, and he spends time with me. We play silly little games—like the time I rigged a bottle cap to hang from the ceiling with tape. Then he and I took turns tossing a tennis ball back and forth to hit the cap. It was silly, but it was fun! He doesn't have much money, but he spends time with me—that is what matters.

Just then, I remember that I haven't told my dad the good news.

"Dad, did I tell you that Reeni bought me some clothes and a pair of shoes?" I ask, my voice a bit louder than I expect—I can barely contain my excitement.

"What? All right!" he says, drawing out the vowels and giving me a high-five. "That was real nice of her. What did she—"

But he's cut off by a question from inside the house. "What? What did you just say, Daijha?" my mom asks as she walks back out onto the porch.

"I said that Reeni bought me some shoes and clothes." I am still so excited that I don't pay any attention to the look that crosses my mom's face.

"Oh, she has money like that?" Mom turns on her heels, snatches the screen door open, and stomps into the house. I hear her fussing about needing money while Reeni is out wasting it. Dad and I look at each other, and he shakes his head. He stands up, pulls his keys from his jeans pocket, and says, "That's my cue. I'll see you later."

"Can I come?"

"Not right now, babe."

"Can I stay the night tonight?"

"Uh ... maybe. I'll either come by or call you later, okay?"

"Yeah." I give him a hug and he kisses my cheek. I watch him walk off. My pops is a few inches taller than me and has chocolate-brown skin and a belly. He also has big brown eyes and dimples in his cheeks when he smiles. Everyone says I look like my dad—except for the belly and dimples. But I get my Kool-Aid smile from my mom.

My dad gets into his brown hoopty and loudly drives away. I know my pops, and I know I'll be staying the night. As long as he doesn't have to work, I know I can talk him into at least that. It is just about making it here for a few hours longer. I don't feel like dealing with mom and her attitude, so I decide to go over Tina's house and see what her crazy self is up to. I walk over, grab the door, and am about to holler in to tell my mom when I hear her voice coming from the back room.

"Yes, you do have some money! Daijha just said you bought her some clothes and shoes, so you need to come by and bring me some ... I don't want to hear that. Bring me some money!" she hollers and slams the phone down.

I suddenly feel so bad. I should have kept my mouth shut about the clothes. I don't want to go over Tina's anymore. I just want to leave—not for a few minutes, but for good. I wish I could be anywhere but here. Why does she have to act like this? She takes the fun out of everything! I sit down on the stairs.

For as long as I can remember, Mom didn't love me as much as she seemed to love Reeni (who's twenty-two) and my brother, Maurice (who's twenty-four). And though she fights with Reeni now, I see the old pictures of Reeni and Reece in nice clothes, smiling. Everybody in the picture looked happy: Mom, their dad, and them—the happy family. Their dad, Michael, paid child support and was the greatest.

Mom mostly spoke good things about him—or at least she didn't speak as negatively about him. But my dad, David, is another story.

According to Mom, David is the sorriest, laziest sack of crap you ever did see. He pays child support, but it is nowhere near what Michael paid for my brother and sister. The only time my mom is cool with Dad nowadays is when he gives her some money or takes me with him.

"Daijha!" Mom's hollering interrupts my thoughts.

"Yes?" I holler right back.

"Come in here and clean this kitchen and straighten up this living room."

I get up from the stairs and head into the house. I should have left when I had the chance. It is going to be a long day.

****

"Ma, what's for dinner?" I ask a few hours later, once I finished cleaning up. Mom is sitting on the couch in her favorite spot reading a book. She's about 5'10" with caramel skin and light-brown eyes—not hazel, just a lighter brown. She has on a pair of blue jeans, a white fitted sweater, and some white slip-on gym shoes. She keeps her hair relaxed and cut short, and right now she has it spiked. When she does smile, it makes a huge difference. Her face lights up, and she looks more like my older sister than my mother. But she isn't smiling now. She looks up at me.

"What do you mean, 'What's for dinner?' Aren't you going to your dad's? He can feed you." She looks back down at her book.

"He already bought me lunch. Plus he isn't coming back for a while."

"Well, wait 'til then." She doesn't even lift her gaze.

"But I'm hungry now. And there is nothing much in the fridge."

"Daijha!" Mom glares up at me. "Look, if you want something now, call your dad. Heck, it's the least he can do with the sorry amount of child support he pays. Stop getting on my nerves with your constant beggin'. If he paid some real child support, I could afford to have food in the house. As a matter of fact"—she slams her book shut and turns toward me—"you should've been worried about that when you were out getting clothes last night. Bet you didn't think about that!" She settles back into the couch and opens her book.

"Forget it! I'm out!" I holler as I slam out the door.

"Uh-uh, Daijha! Get back here and shut my door right!"

But I am already running down the street. I don't look back to see if she comes onto the porch. I'm so sick of her. I mean, dang, I didn't ask to be born. Why does she have to take everything out on me? All she does is yell and holler, unless she's smiling in some man's face.

But it's whatever. One day I'll be gone from her house. I'll move away to go to school in four years, and I can't wait. I'm going to go to school as far away from Ohio as possible.

I turn right at the end of the street and head toward my dad's. I slow to a walk. I am not worried: Mom isn't gonna come after me. She never has—and never will. I'm used to walking to my dad's. It takes me about thirty-five minutes. I like to think on the walk and clear my mind. I also make plans. I'm going to school to be a child psychologist. I'm an A student with an occasional B. I hate Bs, though, and work hard not to get them. All my teachers tell me I'm going to go places. I just pray they're right.

I deal with my home life the best way I can. I deal with school the best way I can. But when home and school are messed up at the same time, I hold on tight to my dreams. When I get really down, I think about all the things I'll be able to do when I go to college and graduate: the friends I'll have, the money I'll have, the husband I will have, the kids and house I will have—how good my life will be. Reeni taught me that. She tells me all the time that things will get better, that I won't always have to stay at Mom's. She tells me to get good grades in school (like she did) and keep focused. A college degree is the key to making it. I believe her. I calm down, remember my dream to be a psychologist, and continue on to Dad's.

As I round the corner to my dad's and look down the street, I see my godfather's motorcycle. He and my dad are sitting on the porch talking. I get closer and they look up. First surprise and then smiles cross their faces.

"Hey, girl!" my godfather shouts out.

"Hey, Uncle P!" I respond, though he's not technically my uncle. He gets up and holds out his arms, and I give him a big old hug. He pulls back, looks at me, and asks, "What are you doing walking across town by yourself?"

I straighten up tall. "Come on, Unc, I'm a big girl. I'm all right."

"Yeah, I guess you are! You got a birthday coming up, huh?"

"Yeah." He knew because we shared the same Zodiac sign: Scorpio.

"Hmmmm … and just how old will you be?"

"Fourteen."

"What?! Real talk? Hey, D," he says, looking back at my dad, acting all surprised, "she said she's gonna be fourteen!" He turns back to me. "Already? Wow! Time is flying."

He sits back down on the porch steps. "Man, D, I remember when you and Janet brought her home from the hospital." I sit down next to him and listen. I love this story. "I was down at the car shop finishing up my shift. I had just wiped off my hands, and you and Janet pulled up with that beautiful little bundle—smooth brown skin with curly black hair and them big ol' cheeks and big brown eyes. Woo man, was she a beautiful baby!" He glances at me and flings his arm around my shoulder. "And getting more beautiful by the minute."

I smile and look down. My godfather always makes me feel special. He used to work at the shop, but now, he owns his own shop. I think he is awesome, not only because he's my godfather and kind of spoils me, but also because he makes me feel special. Uncle Paul looks over at his motorcycle and then nods at me and asks, "You wanna go for a ride?"

"Heck yeah!"

"All right, D, we'll be right back. Cool? You need anything?"

Dad smiles at me and shakes his head no. "I'm good. Just bring my baby girl back safe."

"You already know." Uncle P straps his spare helmet on me, straps on his own helmet, gets on the cherry-red Ninja with silver stripes, steadies it, and helps me get on behind him. I wrap my arms around him and hold on tight. He revs the engine and off we go.

After a thirty-minute ride around town, my uncle pulls back up at my dad's. Pops is still sitting on the porch. I slide off the bike and take off the helmet. Uncle Paul takes out his wallet as I untie my bag of snacks from the back. He pulls out twenty dollars and gives it to me. I strap the spare helmet to the bike, and he hollers "Happy Birthday!" over the noise from the engine. He yells that he loves me, gives me a hug, and drives off. I walk up the steps and sit next to my dad. We sit there quietly for a little while. Dad doesn't ask why I came. He knows.

"I called your mom and let her know you're here" is all he says. I nod and we just sit quietly on the porch. I feel safe.

Chapter 2

"*Beep! Beep! Beep! Beep!*"

Argh, I think. *Time to get up.* I roll over in bed and open one eye to peek at the clock—six thirty on Monday morning already. I smack the clock and roll back over with the dread I usually feel every weekday morning at the arrival of school—until I realize: I have new clothes and shoes to wear!

Suddenly energized, I hop out of bed and head to the bathroom, pull back the shower curtain, and turn on the water. Before I hop in, I grab my rag and look for the bar of soap. Dang! Out of soap again. Man, this is messed up! I cannot go to school in new clothes not smelling fresh.

I look in the mirror. My relaxed black hair reaches just below my ears and flips up slightly. The edges are uneven, and my hair is breaking off. My chocolate-brown skin is dry and doesn't look shiny and healthy like the skin and hair of most of the girls at school. My teeth are at least okay. I look farther down in the mirror. I don't see the curvaceous beginnings of a woman. I see what my mom sees: fat. I am so not cute.

I sigh and head to my mom's room, moving quietly so I don't wake her. I find the soap that she has hidden in her dresser drawer. Today is going to be a good day.

After I shower, brush my teeth, and put mom's soap back, I get dressed. I put on the blue shirt, my blue jeans, and the new canvas shoes Reeni bought me. I comb my hair and mess with it until it looks presentable. I don't bother waking up Mom—she doesn't have to be at work until nine. Her alarm will go off at seven thirty. I'm heading downstairs by seven fifteen. I also don't bother to look in the fridge—I know there is not much there. That's one of two reasons why I leave early for school. One, I can get to breakfast. The pickings at home usually aren't just slim—they're nonexistent. If you can't tell already, food is not a top priority of my mother's. Provision for me, outside of four walls, doesn't seem to be high on her list in general. Sometimes I think she just provides housing because she needs a place to store her clothing.

Anyway, the second reason I leave early and walk is because I hate to ride the bus. Some busta is always fighting and talking crazy to someone. Someone always has to riff on someone else, making fun of their hair, clothes, shoes, face, momma, daddy—the way they talk, the way they breathe … you name it. They are always screaming, and the bus driver is forever stopping the bus.

I much prefer to walk. No noise, no drama. Our neighborhood is relatively safe, and usually there are some other kids walking too. We may not all walk together, but we tend to walk close enough that there is safety in numbers. The walk takes about twenty minutes.

When the school bell rings at 8:10 a.m., I've eaten my breakfast and am headed to homeroom. Ten minutes later, I'm walking down the hall to my first period class, English. I take a deep breath and walk into class. I love school, and I love learning. But I *hate* this particular school. Every day Jerome and Natasha have something to say to or about me—every single day. Now, don't get me wrong. I'm no punk. I can fight. However, they don't fight fair. I've seen them fight, and one of their friends is always trying to jump in. My odds with the two of them and their friends against me are not good. So I try to ignore them—but this doesn't seem to stop them.

"Well, well, well, look who is here." Jerome elbows Natasha.

Natasha hollers, "What? You got some new clothes—go on ahead, girl!" She jumps out of her seat and looks at me in disbelief. You would think that was a compliment, but I know better. Ms. Martell is out in the hall during class change, which means open season on Daijha. As the other kids start to snicker, I slide into my seat and keep my eyes straight ahead. I brace for what is to come. Natasha and Jerome begin to talk to each other. Loudly.

"Her clothes are new," Natasha says as she moves closer to mock-inspect my jeans, "but ... what jeans are those? Lookin' all cheap. And that shirt—they must have been the special!" Natasha looks at Jerome and he starts in.

"Well, at least she has on some Con—OH HOLD UP!" Jerome leans over his desk and looks at my shoes. "Those ain't even Converse! She got conned with that!" They start laughing loudly as the other kids look down at my shoes and start to laugh too.

"Hey, Daijha?" Natasha hollers. "Who conned you into buying those raggedy gym shoes? Whoever—"

"Natasha, it's time to settle down." Ms. Martell has walked into class. She is nice enough and doesn't take any mess. As long as she is in the room, I know they'll keep their mouths shut. Only problem is that she leaves the class often to go into the hall and talk to Mrs. Sanchez from next door. It is during these times that the two will point, talk, and laugh.

After Ms. Martell explains what we are supposed to be doing for the next fifteen minutes, she steps outside to talk with Mrs. Sanchez. The kids start to laugh as Jerome and Natasha start in again. I bristle with anger. I hate Jerome and Natasha. I think of ways that I could get back at them. Violent ways. One-on-one. Fists flying.

"All right, let's go through what we have so far," Ms. Martell says as she walks back into class. We had to read a short story and answer the questions at the end. We trade papers and grade them. I get my paper back and see that I answered all ten correctly. I smile slightly.

Ms. Martell asks for the papers and glances at the scores as we turn them in. "Natasha, what were you doing when you were supposed to be reading? And Jerome?" All eyes turn toward them except mine. I don't even bother looking. I know what they were doing. At least I don't have a class with them again until later. We all have science together, the class before my final class of the day—my favorite class. Art.

I love art. Well, actually, I love to draw. Using pencils and shading is my favorite. Mr. Coya is awesome! All the students in art class seem to get along and just do our work. As I copy down the homework and gather my things, I breathe a sigh of relief that this class is over, looking forward to art.

******

"You are doing very well in here, Daijha. I am impressed! You turn in all your assignments, and you ace every test. You seem to be a natural in math—and I was wondering if I could ask you a favor." Mr. Mathews, my math teacher, has brought me out into the hall during the last few minutes of class and is looking at me expectantly. "I have a few students who need some extra help with math. I am not able to tutor during their study hall, which is the same time as yours. I was wondering if you would consider tutoring them for me? It wouldn't be for long—just a few weeks."

I think for a moment and figure I can pull it off. It doesn't take much to do my homework, and I usually use the rest of my study hall to read. If necessary, I'll do my homework at home. I don't mind helping out. I smile and tell Mr. Mathews I will.

"Great!" He smiles back. "I'll tell Jerome and Natasha I will be able to have them tutored."

My face falls, and I start to shake my head. "No way, Mr. Mathews."

"What? What's the matter?" He looks confused. I'm not a rat, but I can't think of anything else to say that won't make me look bad. And truth is ... I don't care about them. I don't care if they fail every single class!

I look down at my shoes and then look back up and say, "Look, Mr. Mathews, I just can't. We don't get along at all."

He looks as if he were about to say something and then stops. He glances at me for a moment and then says, "Okay, Daijha. Thanks anyway." But I can tell he is disappointed. Dang. The bell rings and the kids start to pile out of the room. Mr. Mathews walks back into the room. I really like Mr. Mathews and don't want him to think less of me. I walk into the room and stand at his desk. He looks up at me.

"Mr. Mathews, they make fun of me all the time," I say quietly. "I just can't do it. Please do not say anything to them." I turn and walk quickly out of the room.

I make it to science class just before the bell and have to walk by Jerome and Natasha to get to my seat. For once, they don't say anything. I am shocked, and, even though I know it's stupid, I quickly glance up at them. They are looking toward the front of the room, and my eyes follow theirs. Two seats in front of me is a new girl. She has light brown skin and dark brown hair down past her shoulders that she has pulled back into a tight ponytail, and she has hoop earrings in her ears. I can only see her from behind, but I can tell she is a really big girl. I'm a "thickums," as they say, with some extra meat on my bones, but she is *really* big. She looks as if she's been stuffed in the desk.

"Good afternoon, y'all. We have a new student joining our class. I know you have been introduced many times today," Ms. Davis says with a smile, "but you have just a couple more to go. I'm sure by now you see some familiar faces, but others are new. So class, this is Jazmyn Bishop. I know you will all be kind in showing Jazmyn the ropes and making her feel welcome."

As Ms. Davis turns to begin with the notes on the board, I hear Jerome loudly whisper, "I know that desk isn't feeling too kind and welcoming!" A few kids start to laugh, and I immediately feel sorry for Jazmyn—until she turns in her desk and pins Jerome with a look that I will never forget. It is a look of complete disdain, not fear. My feelings quickly change from sorrow to admiration.

Before Jazmyn can open her mouth, unfortunately, Ms. Davis, who must have overheard Jerome, kicks Jerome out of class. Dang! I wanted to hear what Jazmyn was going to say!

Once science class is over, I head to art class. I walk in and take my seat near the window. I love art class. The space in the classroom is open, and scattered all over the room are our desks—easel desks that let the top swivel up and down so you can work. They have holders at the bottom that keep our supplies from rolling onto the floor.

I set my things in one of the cubbies under the windows near my desk and take out my supplies. We are working on a still drawing. At the front of the room, some items sit on a table. We have to recreate the image on our canvas using chalk. As I get situated, I see Jazmyn walk in. I think about the look she gave Jerome and smile. She apparently takes it as an invite, 'cause she walks over and sets her books on a desk near mine.

"What's up?" she asks as she looks me up and down.

"Nothing." I give her the same look. She seems to be about the same height as me, but wider. Her face is round. She has dark brown eyes, and she's wearing shiny lip gloss. Her clothes are snug, but they are nice. She's rockin' expensive-looking jeans with a red and pink sweater. She has on a clean pair of pink and red Nikes that match her outfit. She sets her purse down and sits in the desk.

Jazmyn again looks at me. "So what's your name?"

"Daijha."

"Daijha. All right. You already know my name is Jazmyn—I saw you in the last class."

"Yeah."

She smiles. "I'm fourteen. How old are you?"

"Fourteen."

"A'ight. You stay around here?"

"Kinda. I walk, so it takes about twenty minutes."

"Don't they have a bus?"

"Yeah."

She looks at me like I'm crazy. "Well, why don't you take it?"

"Too much drama." I keep my answers simple. She doesn't need to know all of my business. "Where do you live?"

She tells me the name of the street she lives on, which is a couple streets over from mine. I tell her I stay two streets over. She tells me she was going to catch the bus home, but since I am walking, she'll walk with me. I say okay as Mr. Coya is walking over to introduce her to the class and explain what we are doing. I smile to myself because, as corny as it is to be excited, I think I have just met a friend.

Chapter 3

"So did you just move here?" I ask Jazmyn as we head down the stairs and out the doors on our way home from school. She adjusts her backpack and snaps her jacket.

"Yeah. My mom and dad just separated. So we moved out."

"Just you and your mom?"

"Nah. Me, my mom, and my two little sisters."

"Oh. Where did you used to go to school?"

"Paxton," she says.

Paxton is a junior high a few miles away. She tells me that she didn't mind leaving, because it wasn't the best place to be. There were fights all the time, and one kid even brought a gun to school. We have trouble and our share of fights at Mariam, but not like what she was describing. She tells me that her mom decided to move when her mom and dad couldn't stop fighting. She said they loved each other but needed a break.

"Do you miss your dad?" I ask.

"Well, we just moved, and he says he's going to see us all the time, so ..." She shrugs her shoulders. "But I know I don't miss the arguing. Mom crying all the time. Dad always angry."

"Yeah, I hear that."

"What about you? Your mom and dad still together?"

I smack my lips. "Naw! My mom can't stand my dad!" I say, and then I tell her about my mom and dad getting divorced when I was about five. I tell her how I spend as much time with my dad as I can.

"You have any brothers or sisters?" she asks.

"Yeah, one brother and one sister. They are both older than me."

"Okay. This is my street." She points to a house. "You see the yellow house there?" I nod. "That's my house."

"All right. I'll see you later," I say as I head off.

"Hey, wait, Daijha. You walk to school, too?"

"Yeah."

"Well, dang." She sighs. "What time do you start walking?"

"I leave my house at about seven fifteen, seven twenty."

She looks at me, mouth hanging open. "Dang! Why so early?"

I am a little embarrassed when I shrug my shoulders and say, "To eat breakfast."

"Oh. Well, okay."

"All right. Later."

"K. Later."

I finish my walk to the house. I unlock the door, go inside, and toss my book bag on the couch next to the door. It bounces off of the threadbare green plaid couch and bangs onto the dingy beige carpet. I walk by it and head to the kitchen to look in the fridge and see some butter, a swallow of milk in the jug, ketchup, mustard, and a couple eggs. I grab a skillet and put it on the stove, slap in a little butter, and turn on the eye.

As the butter melts, I go back into the living room and turn on the TV. The basic cable is on for now. Thank goodness! I hate when the cable is off. I turn to my favorite teen sitcom and go back to the kitchen to fix my eggs. I crack the two eggs, put them into the skillet, and scramble them up. Once they are finished, I scrape them onto a plate, grab a glass of water and a fork, and head back to the living room. I sit on the couch and watch some TV.

Once I finish my eggs and the show goes off, I take my dishes into the kitchen and put them in the sink. I walk back to the living room, grab my bag, and head to the dining room table. I sit down, pull out my homework, and get started.

******

I hear my mom's key in the door and look up at the clock on the dining room wall. Six thirty. She walks into the house with her work bag and heads toward the stairs and her room.

"Hey, Mom," I say before she reaches the stairs.

"Hey, Daijha." She continues up the stairs to her room.

I give her a few minutes, and when she doesn't come back down, I head up the stairs. As I near the top of the stairs, I hear her crying. I know something is really wrong, because my mom doesn't cry. I peek around the corner and see her holding some envelopes and bills. One looks like the yellow envelope the mortgage bill comes in. I walk the rest of the way up the stairs. I begin toward her room, but she stops me.

"Daijha, go back downstairs."

"Mom, what's the matter?" I walk closer to her room, and she shoves the papers to the bed where I can't see them.

"Go back downstairs, Daijha." I take another step toward her. "Now."

I turn and head down the stairs. I can't remember ever seeing my mom cry and really don't know what to do. She's usually fussing and yelling and spending time with her dude. And I definitely can't remember ever seeing her cry like that. I hear her coming down the stairs, so I go sit at the dining room table.

Mom walks to the door and then stops and turns. "I'll be right back," she says as she grabs her purse and heads out the door. I watch her leave and am not sure she'll be back tonight. For the first time that I can remember, I'm more worried about my mom than angry with her. I don't know what to do. I grab the phone and call my dad.

"Hello?"

"Hey, Dad."

"Hi, baby girl, what's up? How was your day?"

"It was all right, Dad. I met this new girl today, and her name is Jazmyn. She lives a couple streets over."

"Okay! Sounds like you may have a new girl to hang with." Dad worries about me making friends. I'm kind of a loner.

"I might, but I just met her, Dad. She seems straight, though. But Dad, Mom was crying earlier."

"Oh, yeah?" Dad doesn't sound all that concerned. "Why was she crying?"

"I don't know. She was sitting on her bed with, I think, the mortgage bill in her hand, and she was just crying."

The front door opens, and Mom walks in with a bag from the burger shop up the street. I am a little surprised to see her. "Mom's back, Dad. I'll talk to you later, okay?"

"Okay, Dae," Dad says before hanging up.

"Are you hungry, Dae?" Mom asks. "I brought you a burger and fries."

"Thanks, Mom." I go to the table and open the bag. Mom comes back with two cups of water. I see one burger and one order of fries.

"Mom, where is your food?"

"I ate in the car, Dae. How was school?" she asks.

Now, Mom can't stand for anyone to eat in her car. So I know she's lying. I don't keep asking, though—I'm just happy to have something to eat. I offer her half my burger, but she shakes her head no. I sit down and talk to my mom about the day, but I'm more worried than ever. Earlier she was crying, and now she's home talking to me. Something must be up. I decide to call Reeni, as soon as I am alone, and see if she knows anything.

The next morning, I get up, go through my routine, and head out the door. As I'm coming up on Jazmyn's street, I see her waiting at the corner.

"Hey, Daijha. I figure I may as well walk with you and keep you company."

I smile. "That's cool."

She smiles back, and we begin our walk.

Once at school, we pick up our breakfast: a sweet roll, a fruit cup, milk, and orange juice for me, and just an orange juice for her. She says she already ate and walked just to keep me company.

"What is your first class?" I ask Jazmyn on our way to a table.

"English." She opens her orange juice and takes a swallow.

I pause in unwrapping my sweet roll and say, "Oh yeah? With who?"

"Ms. ..." She roots around in her book bag and fishes out her schedule. " ... Martell?"

"Yeah? I do too. You weren't there yesterday." I pull off a piece of the sweet roll and pop it into my mouth.

"Yeah, I know. I came in late. We had to stop in the office, so I missed first period."

"Oh, okay."

"So how is her class? Boring?" J, as she told me to call her, asks before finishing off her orange juice and putting her schedule back into her book bag.

I take my last swig of orange juice and wrap up my trash to throw away.

"No, it's not really boring." I think about Jerome and Natasha, and a familiar sense of dread settles into my stomach.

"You don't sound very excit-" The first school bell cuts her off. In ten minutes, the late bell will ring. We gather up our things, throw away our trash, and step out into the hallway, which is quickly filling up with students. We don't talk on our way to our lockers, not wanting to yell over the noise.

J's locker is across the hall from mine. I grab the books I need from my locker and book bag and then toss my book bag in my locker. I shut the door, spin the lock, and turn around. J is finishing up, and I walk over. She shuts her locker and spins the lock, and we head to our homerooms.

After homeroom, we meet up in the hall in front of Ms. Martell's class. We walk into class, and I go to my desk. Jazmyn doesn't know where to go, so she walks up to Ms. Martell's desk. Ms. Martell looks up at J and smiles.

"Hello. You must be Jazmyn. I'm Ms. Martell. Nice to meet you." She stands up and holds out her hand to Jazmyn. Jazmyn takes her hand and smiles.

"Yes, I am. Nice to meet you too, Ms. Martell."

Ms. Martell walks over to a desk near where Jerome and Natasha sit. Neither is here yet, and I am hoping they are both absent. Those are always good days.

"You may sit here, Jazmyn." Ms. Martell points to a desk two rows over from my seat.

"Thank you," J says as she puts her things under her desk and sits down. The second bell rings. There are four minutes left until the final bell. No Jerome. No Natasha. I look at J, she looks at me, and I point to the board, where the assignment we are supposed to begin is listed. I grab my book and a sheet of paper from under my desk and open the book to the right page.

I'm reading through the material and starting to answer the first question when I hear snickering behind me. I don't have to turn to see who it is. I already know. They must have come in while I was reading. I look down at my new jeans, orange T-shirt, and new blue shoes. I really don't know what they are laughing at—I mean, I look all right. I feel my face get warm as my anger rises. I am so tired of them! I don't mess with them at all. I don't say anything to them. I don't even look at them! But for some reason, every single day, they make it a point to get at me. Why? I know that if I look their way, they are just going to go even stronger. So I don't. Again.

Ms. Martell gets up from her desk to hand back some papers while we are supposed to be working. She stops at James's desk to talk to him about his paper. While she is talking to James, I can hear whispering coming from the back of the room. I make out the words "huge," "fat," and "fit in a desk." Now, I have heard Jerome and Natasha talk about me before, but never about me fitting in a desk. I don't know who they are talking about. I turn to look and see them looking at Jazmyn and snickering. Some of the other kids are starting to laugh.

The laughter causes Ms. Martell, who is at the front of the room, to look up from James and ask, "What is so funny?" She is irritated. She knows Jerome and Natasha well and knows whatever the kids in the back are laughing at is not funny.

I look over at J and see her face turn red. But she turns in her seat and looks at Jerome. "You have something you want to say?"

The other kids quiet down as D'Anthony says, "You gonna let her call you out like that, Jerome? I know I wouldn't. She straight—"

"That's enough, D'Anthony," Ms. Martell barks. "Jerome, step outside."

"What?! I didn't even say anything! Why I gotta go to the hall?" He crosses his arms over his chest, stretches out his legs, and glares at Ms. Martell.

"I know that's right," Natasha chimes in. "We ain't even say anything."

"'We,' Natasha? No one is talking to you," Ms. Martell says. "I need for you to be quiet, or you can join Jerome in the hall."

"Whatever, it ain't no thang. I wasn't doing nothing. You just always want to blame me and Jerome," Natasha responds.

Ms. Martell tosses the papers on her desk and heads toward the door. She opens the door and waits, but neither Natasha nor Jerome move.

"Either you come out here willingly so we can talk, or I'll have someone go and get Mr. Brown and he can handle it."

Mr. Brown is the principal, and he is no joke. He isn't huge like an NFL lineman, but he isn't small either. He is somewhere in the middle, maybe 5'10" with muscles. He isn't skinny and he isn't fat. His hair is neatly cut in a close fade with a little bit of gray. Even when he smiles, he looks very serious, though he does not yell. He doesn't even raise his voice.

I don't know what it is about him that makes kids listen, but they do. I have seen kids yelling and hollering and talking crazy to each other and to teachers. Then, Mr. Brown takes them into his office one at a time. They go in acting crazy and come out either crying with their heads down or just quiet with their heads down. Either way, they do not come out the same way they went in.

Again, I don't know what he does. And I don't want to know. But I do know that, I—and most everyone else with any sense at this school—ain't trying to go see him. Natasha and Jerome do have some sense. They get up out of their seats and go to the hall.

They come back into the class looking real angry, but they don't say anything else. Ms. Martell finishes passing out papers and begins class. When the bell rings, Jerome and Natasha are two of the first ones out the door. I'm thankful that I don't have to see them again until science, but I feel bad because I know they have a new target. You'd think I'd be happy that their stupidity is no longer aimed at me. And truthfully, I am. But I know how it feels to be on the other side of their comments, and … I feel sorry for Jazmyn. She doesn't know what she is in for.

Chapter 4

"You okay?"

Jazmyn and I are walking towards our next classes. Hers is math and mine is social studies, but they are a couple doors down from each other.

Jazmyn actually smiles. "Yeah. I'm good."

"Those two are idiots," I say. "They think they are hilarious, always running their mouths."

J shrugs her shoulders. "I'm kind of used to it. I have heard it all: 'huge,' 'fats,' 'fatty' ... 'Dang, what do you eat?!' 'Dang, let me hide my lunch!'" She shakes her head. "Kids will shake when I walk by, like I'm so big it causes the ground to shake. And those are the cleaner versions." J sighs.

"Doesn't that make you mad?" I ask, thinking of how it makes me feel when they talk about me.

She nods her head. "Yeah, I'll be honest. It does sometimes. It hurts my feelings. But then I think about who I am and Whose I am, and it gets me through."

"What do you mean, 'whose I am'?" I figure she means her mom and dad support her and make her feel good about herself. But the bell rings before Jazmyn can answer. I won't see her again until science.

The rest of the day passes, and I am waiting for Jazmyn by our lockers. She wasn't in science or art and I don't know what happened to her. I hope she didn't go home early. She didn't seem sick earlier. But I know if someone would have picked me up early on some of the days Natasha and Jerome were particularly nasty, I would have left. I decide to give it a few more minutes before I start walking.

After a bit, Jazmyn comes around the corner and spots me. As she starts to walk over, Jerome and a couple boys block her path. Jerome steps right in front of her.

"So you didn't hear me in class this morning, and you wanted me to repeat myself," Jerome says loud enough for everyone nearby to hear.

I glance around the hall to see if there are teachers nearby. There are, but they are farther down the hall. I see Jazmyn stand up straighter and look Jerome in the eye, but she doesn't say anything. She just stands there as if waiting for him to continue.

I move through the growing crowd to get closer to her. I don't know what's about to happen, but I want to be there for whatever does.

Jerome is looking at her with a smirk on his face. He's tall and dark brown. He has brown eyes and a close-cut fade with a swirling design on the side, and he stays dressed in the hottest gear: crisp, baggy blue jeans with gold stitched designs on the pocket, an oversized gold T-shirt, a matching oversized gold jacket, and bright white gym shoes. His arms are crossed over his chest.

Jerome is on the basketball team, and I notice that the boys he has with him are on the team too. They follow Jerome around like he's some kind of god and hang on to his every word. They all feed off each other and act like a pack of hungry wolves. They smell fresh blood in the air and are licking their lips at the prospect of prey.

"Yeah, I heard you tried to front on Rome this morning," one of the beasts says. He looks Jazmyn up and down. "Now you know you shouldn't be frontin' on nobody at all!"

The kids milling around start to laugh and, sensing something is about to jump off, move in closer. Jerome takes it as his cue to go in for the kill.

"What I said was 'How in the world did she fit in the desk? She knows good and well that desk wasn't reinforced to support all that!'"

The laughter is deafening. I move in and stand next to her. For one of the first times I can remember, I don't drop my head; I look at Jerome too. I don't know where the strength came from, and I don't know what I am going to say, but as I open my mouth to say something, I hear a quiet but strong voice beside me.

"Are you finished? Do you feel better? You finally have my undivided attention." I turn and look at Jazmyn. Her voice is strong and sure. And she is ... smiling!

"Dang, Jerome!" She shakes her head and continues with a smirk, all while maintaining eye contact with him. "Why you sweatin' me? For real, you must like all that you see, 'cause you have made it your point to get at me. I just got here, and for two days you have been at it! And now you even brought your friends! Okay, okay." She opens her notebook, scribbles something in the corner of a page, and it rips off. "I'll give you my number!"

Jazmyn winks, and as she pushes by an open-mouthed Jerome, she shoves the paper into his jacket pocket. "Later, Jerome."

She looks over her shoulder and says, "Come on, Dae."

Jerome isn't the only one with his mouth open. I quickly close mine and follow Jazmyn through the crowd. I look over my shoulder and see many other open mouths and more than a few looks of admiration. I think I even saw admiration cross Jerome's face when he turned as we passed.

"Man, whatever!" he hollers halfheartedly. "Don't *nobody* want your number!" A few hangers-on laugh, but everyone else turns back to getting ready to leave.

Chapter 5

I'm still in shock as Jazmyn and I gather our things and begin our walk home. I don't think I could have ever said those things to Jerome. I can't stand him and wanted to stand up for myself, but I was not looking forward to how he would have responded. I thought he and Natasha might get nastier or even jump me. But they didn't do any of that to J. She stood up for herself, and it worked!

"J, that's what's up! The way you stood up to Jerome—GIRL!" I say. I smack my fist into my hand, turn, and walk backward in front of her, talking excitedly.

"Where did you get that from? I don't think I ever could have stood up to him. Before you came, he used to get on me all the time. Him and Natasha. I used to ignore them, but that didn't seem to help at all. But what you did ..."

Jazmyn smiles. "It wasn't all that, Dae." She isn't nearly as pumped I am.

"Really, J. I mean, really." I stop walking, making her stop too. I look her in the eye, and she returns my gaze—and then we both double over laughing.

"I guess it was funny, though!" Jazmyn says between laughs. "Did you see the look on his face? It was too funny!"

"Girl, his jaw was scraping the ground!"

"Yes, it was!"

We compose ourselves, and I fall in step beside her as we start walking again.

"You think he's going to say anything crazy tomorrow?" I ask J as we break into our separate thoughts.

She shrugs her shoulders. "I don't know. He might … but I don't really care, Dae." I look at her closely, and it seems like she really doesn't. I am amazed but don't quite believe her.

I raise my eyebrow. "Really, J? It won't bother you if he has something crazy to say? Or worse, if he and his goons are wai-"

Jazmyn stops midstride, raises one hand, and looks me in the eye as she interrupts me. "Dae, I'm serious. It really doesn't matter. You know earlier, when I said I know Whose I am?"

I nod my head yes.

"Well, I do. I'm God's child, and He is with me no matter what. He strengthens me when I can't be strong for myself. Do you go to church, Daijha?"

"Sometimes," I say, not knowing where she is going with this.

"Where do you go?"

"Jerusalem Church with my dad sometimes. I used to go to Saint James with my mom," I tell Jazmyn. When my brother, sister, and I were younger, Mom used to take us to church all the time. My dad and I just started going to his church recently, but we only go once a month at best.

"Well, then, do you believe in God?" Jazmyn asks. I nod. "Then you should know that you are a child of God. Have you been saved?"

I am not too sure, so I shrug my shoulders. "I don't know."

"You should come to church with me sometimes ... if it's ok with your parents. We have so much fun!" Jazmyn smiles.

"What do you do at church?" I have been to church, and it is okay. But "fun"? I wouldn't use that word.

"Lots of stuff. You should come to church with me Sunday. You want to?"

"Sunday is my birthday."

"For real? You didn't tell me. How old are you going to be? Fifteen?"

"No. Fourteen."

"But I thought you said you were fourteen already." J looks at me quizzically.

I shrug. "Well, it was only a few days away, so I just said fourteen."

This was mostly the truth, but a small part was that I just said it because she was already fourteen. I didn't want to sound like I was a baby, so I just said fourteen too. It all seems so silly now that I know how cool she is.

"Oh, okay. Well, what are you doing for your birthday? You having a party?"

"No. We usually don't do anything too big," I say, glad she dropped the age questions. My mom usually takes me out to eat or something. No big deal. Sometimes, my dad takes me to get something nice. Who knows, though? With the way my mom was crying, there's no telling what is going to happen.

"Oh, okay. Hey, you want to come over?" Jazmyn asks.

"Na. I gotta be home when my mom gets there."

"Well, how about tomorrow? You can ask tonight, and she can pick you up from over here tomorrow."

I think for a moment and then nod.

"Okay. That sounds good. I'll ask her tonight and see."

"Well, call me tonight and let me know. Let's exchange numbers." J pulls out her phone, and I tell her my number. I don't have a cell phone, so I write her number in my notebook. I stuff the notebook back in my bag and sling it over my shoulder.

"All right, Dae. I'll see you in the morning."

"All right. See ya."

When I get to my house, I call my dad to let him know I am home and eat a bowl of cereal for snack. My mom bought some groceries yesterday evening. After we talked, she called my dad, and she went upstairs so I couldn't hear the conversation. About an hour later, my dad came over and gave my mom some money, and she went to the store and bought some breakfast food and things for dinner.

I decide to surprise her and cook dinner tonight. It seems like we are getting along better. She has stayed home the past couple days and is doing a lot less yelling. However, she seems to be so sad.

I haven't had a chance to talk to my sister. I called yesterday while my mom was gone, and Renni wasn't home. When I called her cell, it went to voice mail. I didn't leave a message 'cause she doesn't check them anyway. So for now, I'll just be happy that Mom's home and cook her dinner.

I learned to cook from watching my mom. When she cooks, she can throw down! She cooks a mean lasagna, beef stroganoff, and baked spaghetti. She *kills* chicken (any way she cooks it!), pork chops, and fish. Her scalloped potatoes, potato salad, greens, macaroni and cheese, green beans, and cabbage are off the charts. She hasn't really cooked like that in a very long time, but just thinking about it makes me want Thanksgiving to hurry up. But for now, I'll settle for making some hamburgers and fries.

When Mom gets home, I'm just taking the fries out of the oven and setting them on top. The burgers are finished and are waiting on a plate on the counter next to the stove. Mom walks into the kitchen.

"Hey, Dae, I thought I smelled something good," she says. She walks over to the sink and washes her hands.

"Hey, Mom. How was your day?" I ask. I grab two plates and two cups out of the cupboard. I set them on the table and go grab some silverware, bread, ketchup, mustard, and mayonnaise. Mom brings the burgers and fries to the table.

"It was okay. How was school?" she asks.

I fill the cups with ice and fruit punch. "Man Mom, you will not believe what J—"

"J?" Mom interrupts.

"Yeah, Mom, J. Jazmyn? The girl I told you I met?" I try to jog Mom's memory. I told her about J, but she was probably thinking about other things.

"Oh yeah," she says. "I remember. Go ahead."

As we fix our plates and eat, I tell mom all about how Jazmyn stood up for herself. Mom's eyes widen, she nods her head appreciatively, and a small smile parts her lips. She is impressed.

I've never really told her too much about Jerome and Natasha messing with me. I started to at the very beginning of the year, and she just told me to stand up for myself. She was irritated when I told her a second time and asked me what I wanted her to do. Since I wasn't really sure myself, I just stopped talking to her about it.

After we finish talking about school, I ask her about work. She says that it's going well and tells me about the people she has to deal with at the nursing home. She is a nurse aide in an Alzheimer's unit, and she had plenty of funny stories to tell. She always told me that the disease itself isn't funny and that it is very hard on the families. But some of the residents do some funny things. They can be as sweet as pie one minute and mean as nails another.

As we finish eating, I ask Mom the question I have been waiting to ask. I know she doesn't want me to, but I am going to ask it anyway. I take a deep breath.

"Mom, why were you crying yesterday?" I hold my breath. I don't want to ruin our good evening and conversation, but

I'm worried about her. Mom looks at me, and I can tell she is torn—she doesn't want to tell me.

I let my breath out. "Please tell me, Mom. Are you okay?"

"Yes, Dae, I'm fine." Mom sighs. "There is nothing that you need to worry about."

She gets up to start clearing the table. I get up to help. I know she isn't telling me the truth, but I also know that if I pressure her, she will get angry and might start yelling and carrying on. I like this Mom who came home and spent time with me. I don't want to make her mad.

I put the condiments and bread back, and she put the dishes in the sink. She turns on the hot water and starts to make dishwater.

"Mom, can I go over to Jazmyn's house after school tomorrow? She invited me over and said that I could stay there until you get home."

"Where does she stay?"

"Two streets over."

"Who does she live with?"

"Her mom and sisters."

"What's her mom's name?"

"Uhhh … I think she said Doris."

"Do you have her number?"

"Yes."

"Well, call her so I can talk to her mother. After I speak with her, if everything is okay, then it should be all right."

I smile—partly because I get to go over Jazmyn's, and partly because my mom wants to check and see if it is okay.

It has been a long time since it felt like my mom cared, and I like it.

I go get the phone and call Jazmyn. When she answers, I tell her what my mom said, and she puts her mom on the phone. I tell my mom I'll wash the dishes and clean the kitchen, and I give her the phone. She dries her hand on a dishtowel and heads to the living room.

When Mom comes back into the kitchen, I'm almost finished with cleaning. I wipe down the counters before sweeping the floor.

"Thanks for cleaning the kitchen, Dae. It looks good. You can go over Jazmyn's tomorrow. Her mom seems like good people." She pauses. "You didn't tell me her mom and dad are separated," she adds, looking off in the distance for a moment.

"I hope they can work it out," she says before walking out the kitchen and going upstairs.

When Mom is home, this is her unwind time. She goes up and takes a shower and reads a little. She might come back downstairs; she might not. I settle down on the couch to watch some TV before I go to sleep.

It's about ten when I hear Mom holler down and tell me it's time for bed. I shut off the TV, make sure all the doors and windows are locked, and go upstairs. Mom is sitting on her bed with papers and envelopes spread all over. She pushes them to the side as I stop at her door to tell her good night. She tells me good night, sadness in her voice and on her face. Now I'm really worried.

I tell Mom I forgot something, and turn and go down the stairs. When I get down there, I grab the phone off the base and quickly dial my sister. No more putting it off.

"Hello?" Reeni asks guardedly, no doubt because she saw Mom's number scroll across her screen and didn't know which one of us was calling.

"Hey, Reeni."

"Hey, Nee! What's up? Why are you calling so late?"

I dive right in. "Something's wrong with Mom."

"What? What's the matter? Where is she? Is she hurt? Is she breathing? Is she—"

"Reeni, calm down! Not like that."

"Daijha, what is going on?" Reeni is irritated now.

"Look, Reeni, I didn't mean to get you upset. Dang! I'm just worried about Mom. She has been really sad lately. She's even staying home and spending time with me."

Reeni is exasperated. "Well, what's wrong with her spending time with you?"

"Come on, Reeni. Mom hasn't stayed home in a minute. And she was crying."

"Oh." Reeni knows Mom does not cry.

"I asked her myself, Reeni, but she won't tell me." I know Reeni is probably still mad at mom about how Mom talked to her. But Reeni doesn't hold grudges.

"All right, I'll call her tomorrow. Now go to bed," she chides.

I smile. "All right, Reeni. Good night."

"Good night."

I hang up the phone and go back upstairs. As I turn to go to my room, Mom calls out from her room, "What took you so long?"

"Um ... I called Dad to tell him good night before he went into work," I lie.

"All right. Good night."

"Good night, Mom."

Chapter 6

"So ... what are you going to say to Jerome and Natasha today when they start in on you?" I ask J on our way to school the next day.

The temperature can be up and down in November, and today, it is quite chilly out. I have on a simple black waist-length coat, thin gray gloves, and a fuzzy black scarf. J is bundled up in a heavy lime and blue jacket, lime gloves, blue ear warmers, and a blue scarf. I laugh when I first see her. She doesn't think it is funny at all and rolls her eyes.

"I'm not going to be walking much longer. Girl, I hate the cold!" J says. "Either my mom or dad is going to start taking me in the mornings. You're welcome to ride along if you want to."

"Will you still go a little early so I can get breakfast?"

J smiles. "Sure! As long as my mom and dad don't mind."

"All right, then. I'll ask my mom tonight and let you know."

"Cool."

"So back to Jerome and Natasha. What do you think you'll say to them?"

"I don't think I'm going to have to say much, if anything," J responds.

"Why do you say that? Don't you think he'll have something to say after what went down yesterday? You shut him down."

J shrugs her shoulders. "You know, most of the time, when I stand up to people, they leave me alone. It really depends on how you talk to them. I talked to my mom and dad about it the other day, and they both told me to stand up for myself. But they don't just stop with that. They told me what he might be feeling and why he might be doing it, what some right responses might be, and to pray about it. I listened to what they said and prayed"—she shrugs again—"and that is what came out."

"You prayed, and those words came out just like that?"

J smiles. "Kind of. I wasn't scared of him, Dae, or what he might do. I wasn't afraid of the crowd, either. It just felt right to say those words at that time. I'm not embarrassed about who I am or ashamed."

I don't know what else to say. I don't know any kids who talk like this, including my friend Tina. Tina and I have been cool for a while, but we don't hang out much. She goes to a different school, and she spends most of her time at her grandma's a few miles away. Before, we used to get together on the weekends when she would be home, but now, she doesn't even come home on the weekends. It has been weeks since we saw each other.

J and I finished the rest of our walk to school quietly, caught up in our thoughts.

J was right—Jerome didn't have anything to say about or to her today. Natasha wasn't there. He just ignored her. J ignored him too. She wasn't mean or nasty. She just didn't pay him any mind.

On our way home, I tell J that she was right about Jerome leaving her alone.

She smiles and says, "Thank God! He came through for me. This may not be the end of it, but God is looking out for me, and I'll be fine."

I don't know what to say—I never hear kids talking about God like they know Him personally—so I just change the subject and ask her about what we are going to do when we get to her house.

"Well, we'll eat something and get to homework." She turns to me. "You have any homework?"

I nod.

"Cool. So after homework, a few of my friends from my church youth group are coming over. We'll all just hang out in the front room and laugh and talk until about seven thirty."

"Oh," is all I say. I start to get a familiar, sick feeling in the pit of my stomach. I didn't think there would be other kids there. I'm very shy, and I'm always uncomfortable when I meet new people.

Even though we have only known each other a short while, J is able to pick up on my mood shift and realize I'm not really feeling it. "It will be cool, Dae. They are all straight. It is my week to host our youth group, and you are my friend, so I want you to be there too."

"All right," I say. I am nervous as to how they will treat me, but I am hoping that it won't be that bad.

The closer we get to her house, the more nervous I become. I hate meeting new people. By the time we walk up the steps to her house, I feel sick to my stomach. We walk in the front door and I quickly look around. We are standing in the family room. It is clean and the furniture is used, but not raggedy—more comfortable-looking. There are two rust-colored couches and a matching armchair. The television is on a stand in the corner, and there is a throw rug on top of the hardwood floor. Everything matches. It is nice, cozy. J's mom comes in from another room.

"Hi, baby girl," she says to J as she gives her a big hug. She turns to me and smiles. "You must be Daijha," she says, holding out her arms to me. I hesitate for a moment—my family doesn't hug. But she continues to hold out her arms and smile warmly. I walk into her arms and she gives me a hug too. It's funny, but it didn't feel awkward—it felt nice.

"Yes," I say quietly.

She smiles even bigger. "No need to be shy, Daijha. I won't bite!" She laughs and J does too. I just smile a little. "Alright. My name is Doris, as I'm sure Jazmyn told you. You can call me Ms. Doris, or Ms. D for short. Okay?"

I nod my head yes.

"Y'all go put your things in Jazmyn's room and then come and get a snack before you start on your homework," she says as she goes back to the room she came from.

Ms. Doris is a taller, older version of Jazmyn. She is a big woman too, but since she stands about six inches taller than Jazmyn, she looks thinner.

I follow Jazmyn up the stairs to her room. J's room is also neat and clean. She has a full-size bed with a purple geometric print comforter and matching pillow. Her dresser is a light wood color. The walls are painted lavender, and there is a diamond-shaped mirror over her dresser. There are several picture frames on top. I put my book bag on the floor next to her bed and pick up a couple picture frames. She leans in next to me.

"That's me and my dad." She already told me her dad's name is Daniel. He is taller than her with dark brown skin. His hair is curly and pulled back into a ponytail. He has hazel eyes and a big grin on his face and has one arm slung over J's shoulder.

There is another picture of her, her mom, her dad, and two little girls. One girl looks a lot like her dad, and the other—she looks like her mom and her dad. Jazmyn points to the darker-skinned little girl. "That's my sister Maya, and that one"—she points to the other girl—"is my sister Denae."

I set the pictures down and point to the last one. "Who is in this picture with you?" I ask.

"These are a few of my friends from my youth group—David, Andre, Adam, Maria, Rashonna, and Meeka," she says, pointing each of them out in the picture.

"Come on, let's wash our hands and go eat," Jazmyn says, leading me to the bathroom.

I am hungry and ready for a snack so I quickly wash my hands and follow her back downstairs. Jazmyn's little sisters are at the table munching away on some cereal.

"Hey, J," they mumble around mouthfuls of food. "Who's that?"

"It's rude to talk with your mouth full," their mom says. "And you don't say 'Who's that?' You either wait for your sister to introduce her, or you introduce yourself first."

Both girls continue to look at me curiously. "Yes, ma'am," they say in unison.

I smile. They are cute. Jazmyn turns to me. "These are my sisters, Maya and Denae, and you two"—she turns back to the girls—"this is my friend Daijha."

"Hey!" Maya yells excitedly. "I have a Daijha in my class, too!"

"Me, too!" hollers Danae.

Maya smacks her lips and says, "No you don't!"

"Yes I do! Yes I do!"

"Whatever. You always say the same thing I say." She rolls her eyes. "You don't even go to a real school, anyway."

"Yes I do!" Denae is beginning to tear up and her voice starts to quiver. She hops up from the table and runs over to her mom. She gets to Ms. Doris, grabs her legs, and starts to cry.

Ms. Doris bends over and picks Denae up.

"Ssh," she coos while she pats Denae's back.

She turns to Maya. "Maya, number one, she does go to school. Yes, it is preschool, and she only goes for a few hours a day, but it is still school. And two, how do you know if she has a Daijha in her class?"

Maya's arms are crossed and she is scowling down at the table.

"Maya?" Ms. Doris says firmly. She is talking in her mom voice—that voice that lets you know she isn't playing.

"I don't," Maya grudgingly admits. But she doesn't look up or take the scowl off her face.

"Well, then, maybe you shouldn't have said anything to her. What do you think?" She sets Denae down at the table and turns back to the counter. Denae begins munching on her cereal and looks at Maya. Maya doesn't answer. I look at Ms. Doris, who has washed her hands and is drying them off on a dishtowel. She turns around to face Maya. Whoa! The look on her face! She looks like my mom does when she is about to get at me!

The room falls silent and Maya looks up. She sees her mom approaching with that look and quickly answers her mom. "No, Ma, I shouldn't have."

Maya looks like she wants to run. I glance up at Jazmyn, who is trying not to laugh, and then back at Ms. Doris, who has stopped moving toward Maya. Before she turns back to the counter, she looks Maya in the eye.

"Don't play with me, Maya. You already know you don't like what happens when you do, right?"

"Yes," Maya quietly agrees.

"All right then." She turns back to the counter to finish mixing what looks like meatloaf.

"You two," she instructs Jazmyn and me, "can eat in the dining room."

"Okay," Jazmyn and I say in unison.

While the girls were arguing, Jazmyn had warmed some pizza rolls and poured two cups of fruit punch. I carry the glasses into the dining room, and she brings the plate of food. We sit down at the table, look at each other, and start laughing.

"How old are they again?" I ask.

"Maya is eight going on twenty-five, and Denae is four," J answers around bites of her pizza rolls.

I laugh and finish the roll I am chewing. "That was funny! They were going at it!"

"I know," J says. "They do it all the time."

"Your mom looks like she doesn't play."

"And she don't! That's what gets me about Maya. She knows mom will bust her behind, but she will still keep runnin' that mouth. I'm like, 'Dang, Maya, be quiet already!' But she won't. But then, when mom gets mad ... oh, then Maya'll start crying and stuff. I'm like, 'Why you crying now?'"

I laugh. I think for a second about what it would be like to have a little brother or sister. I always wanted one, but it never happened. I know some kids can't stand having younger brothers and sisters, but I think it would be fun. It would at least be less lonely.

After we finish up our snack, we take the plate and cups back into the kitchen. Daijha places them in the sink, and we head upstairs to do our homework. J tells me I can sit at the desk, and she sits on her bed. We open up our book bags and get down to business.

It is nice not being at home alone doing homework. We talk back and forth about different things. Boys. Clothes. Her church. Boys. We are laughing about one boy in particular when her mom opens the door a crack and peeks around it.

"It sounds like you're having too much fun to actually be getting any work done," she jokes.

"We're doing good, Mom. I think we're almost finished?" Jazmyn looks at me questioningly.

I nod. "Yes, I'm almost finished. I just have a couple more math problems to do."

Ms. Doris smiles and nods. "Okay, then. Your crew will be here shortly."

J's mom shuts the door. I finish my math problems and put my books in my bag. J puts her books back in her bag too and straightens her bed.

"When my crew comes over, we sit downstairs. Since there are boys in the group, we aren't allowed to be up here. We have to sit where we can be seen," J explains.

"Why?"

"It's a respect thing and keeps us honest. We won't be tempted to be inappropriate in any way."

I nod, grab my book bag, sling it over my shoulder, and we go downstairs. I set my bag near the door so I won't have to look for it when my mom comes. It is about five thirty, and my mom will be here at about six thirty. Ms. Doris calls J and me to place some snacks on the dining room table. There are cookies, apple slices, and bottles of juice. While we set out the food, J explains what they do in their group.

"We talk a little and catch up. We tell each other about the good things that have been going on and sometimes the not-so-good. We'll catch up over snacks for about thirty minutes, and then we'll have Bible study. We all have Bibles and workbooks, and we'll do a lesson in our workbooks. My mom will stay close by, and if we have any questions, we can ask her. She also listens, and if we get off track with a thought, then she'll help get us back on track." I nod and listen quietly. J continues, "Like I said before, we go to each other's houses, and our parents take turns observing. Once every few weeks, we all meet with our pastor. He checks our work, asks us questions, and answers any questions we have."

At about 6:00 p.m., the doorbell rings, and J's friends begin to trickle in. J introduces me to everyone. They range in age from twelve to fourteen. We sit around her dining room table, and they share stories about their week. When it is my turn, I look down. My shyness takes over. I feel silly, but I can't make myself talk. My cheeks burn and the tips of my ears are hot. Why can't they just skip me? I shrug my shoulders.

"Come on," Adam encourages me, "there has to be something that happened that is good."

I look up, and they are all smiling at me—I mean, real smiles. They aren't ready to attack and make fun of me. They are all cool. Suddenly, I don't feel quite as shy.

I shrug my shoulders again before saying, "I met a new friend this week, who introduced me to some more new friends."

I know it's corny, but hey, it's the truth. Rashonna, who is sitting beside me, throws up her hand for a high five and hollers, "All right!" My smile can't be contained. I slap a high five and we all laugh.

The doorbell rings, interrupting the small celebration. I am beginning to have fun and don't realize the time. I look up at the wood clock on the wall and see that it's 6:35 p.m.

Ms. D gets up from the couch and walks to the door. The younger girls are watching a movie on the TV. I get up and begin to clean my area. Ms. D sees me and tells me to relax for a few more minutes.

She opens the door and my mom is standing there. "Hello, Ms. Compton! Come on in." My mom steps through the door and Ms. D opens her arms. My mom looks startled for a second and then gives her a hug. Ms. D steps back and says, "I'm Doris, Jazmyn's mother. We spoke on the phone."

"Hello, Doris." My mom smiles. "And please, call me Janet."

"Okay, Janet. Do you have a couple minutes for a cup of tea?"

Again, my mom hesitates for a second but then agrees. "Yes, I can spare a few minutes."

Mom and Ms. D turn to walk to the kitchen, and Ms. D introduces her to the girls, Jazmyn, and the other kids. They continue into the kitchen and Ms. D calls over her shoulder, "I'll only keep your mom a few minutes, Daijha."

"Okay," I say, wondering what they are going to talk about in the kitchen. I turn back to the group.

Chapter 7

Ms. Doris is true to her word. She and Mom come out of the kitchen after about ten minutes. When Mom and Ms. Doris went to the kitchen, the group took out their Bibles and workbooks. Andre said a prayer and then they began their work. I just listened. Eventually, my mom came out and we left.

As we walk to the car, Mom asks how it went.

"It was good, Mom. The other kids are cool, and their group was interesting. How was work?"

"It was fine. That's good that you had a good time."

We get in the car, and during the short ride home, we don't talk anymore.

Once in the house, Mom sets her workbag and purse down on the couch, walks directly to the kitchen, and starts dinner. I set my book bag by the door and turn and head up the stairs. I take off my school clothes and change into house clothes—my old blue cotton shorts and a faded pink T-shirt. When I came down stairs, Mom has already put some hot dogs and baked beans on the stove.

Mom turns to me. "Watch these while I go upstairs and change."

Once the food is finished, my mom and I sit down to dinner. Mom puts some ketchup on her hot dog and then looks up at me.

"Your sister called me and told me you were worried about me. She said you saw me crying."

I look down at my food and mumble, "Yeah."

I look up with concern in my voice. "What's the matter, Mom? You can talk to me."

Mom looks at me as if wondering if I really can handle it. Her eyes get wet and she looks like she's about to cry. She gets up from the table and goes to the refrigerator. She doesn't get anything from inside; she just opens and shuts the door. She turns around and stares at me as she leans against the wooden doorframe separating the dining room from the kitchen.

She takes a deep breath. "Daijha, they are cutting back hours at work. My hours haven't been cut yet, but now they are talking about laying people off."

"What?" I ask, shocked.

"Yes, Daijha. I could lose my job." She sighs deeply and sits down.

"I can't believe this." I begin thinking of ways I can cost my mom less money. "Mom, we don't have to do anything for my birthday. I'm good. We can cut back—"

Mom sighs and shakes her head. "No, Daijha. It is not your responsibility to worry. I don't want you to worry about it, and that's why I didn't tell you."

"But Mom, we're in this together." I get up, walk over, and stand in front of her.

Mom put her hands on my shoulders and looks me in the eye. "Daijha, you are the child, and I am the mother. I raised both your sister and your brother, and they turned out pretty well, and I'll do the same with you. I just wanted to let you know, in case you've been wondering why I've been acting so funky lately. This is why."

"It's okay, Mom."

I look forlornly at my food. I don't have much of an appetite anymore. Mom doesn't seem to either. She walks over and begins clearing the table.

I join her, lost in thought until Mom's voice breaks in.

"Daijha, don't worry. I'll figure this out."

Mom walks to the kitchen and puts the dishes in the sink. She takes the rag and wipes off the table, and I start some dishwater.

"Mom, Jazmyn asked me to come to church this Sunday."

She stops wiping and looks up at me. "Doris asked me too."

"You want to go?"

Mom hesitates. "I don't know, Dae ..." Mom has been going to Saint James's her whole life. She hasn't gone much lately, but it's the only place she's ever gone. Plus, it's my birthday, and I know she may have some plans for me.

"Mom, it's okay if we go to church. Maybe we could do this instead of dinner for my birthday."

I really don't mind. I haven't had a party for my birthday in ages and don't really want one. And now that my mom might lose her job, I really don't want to spend any extra money on dinner out. It will also be cool to be around Jazmyn and her friends on my birthday.

"I'll think about it," Mom says.

****

"Daijha, are you ready?" Mom calls from her room.

"Almost." I smooth my faded black jersey dress, the only dress I have. I slip on my black flats and go to the bathroom to check my hair. I flipped the edges up earlier, and it looks okay. Mom and I decided to go to church with Jazmyn and her family. I am excited but a little scared. I've gone to church with my dad, but it was more like a chore, like we needed to do it every now and again for things to be okay.

Jazmyn and her mom are different, though. For them, church is more than just a place. They are excited to go and be involved.

"I'm ready, Mom," I call from the bathroom before heading downstairs and sitting down on the couch to wait. Mom comes downstairs dressed in a brown skirt and sweater set and brown heels. She looks really nice. She picks up her purse and keys. I stand up to follow her, and she turns towards me. She frowns slightly at first, real quick, but then smiles and says, "You look nice, Daijha. You ready to go?"

"Yeah." I think of my mom's frown and look down at my outfit.

"What's wrong, Mom? I saw that look on your face."

Mom pauses. "Nothing, Dae." She pauses. "Is that your only dress?"

"Yes, Mom, it is. I don't have all the nice clothes you do!"

I know I snapped, but she hurt my feelings. I at least look presentable. It isn't my fault that she has nice clothes and I don't. If my own mom thinks I look a mess, well, then, why go? Mom looks shocked by my words, but I don't care.

"You know, forget it. I don't want to go anymore. Just go without me!" I turn, run back up the stairs to my room, and slam the door.

As I lie down on my bed, I hear my mom come up the stairs and then the knocking on my door. I'm not even angry, just sad. It hurts that she looked at me that way.

"Go away, Mom. I'm all right."

"Daijha, I'm coming in." I sigh loudly and turn to face the wall.

"Daijha ... I'm—I'm sorry. I didn't mean to hurt your feelings."

"You didn't. I'm good." I mumble, since my face is in my pillow. I don't want her to see me crying.

Mom sighs. "Dae, I know you. You're my baby girl and I know you're crying because I hurt your feelings. Look at me."

I don't budge. Mom gently grabs my shoulders and pulls, "Look at me, Dae."

I turn over to look at her. My eyes are still watery, but I won't let any more tears fall.

Mom sighs again as she rubs my cheek. She sits down on the bed with her back against my stomach. She looks down for a long minute.

"I haven't been doing my best by you, have I?" She raises her head, turns slightly, and looks me in the eye. Her own eyes are watery. I am shocked. I have wanted my mom to realize this for a long time. I've wanted her to apologize to me and beg for my forgiveness. I've wanted it so bad.

But now, when I can see the sadness in my mom's eyes and her own tears ready to fall—no words will come out. She must've taken my silence as confirmation, because she turns her head back and her tears begin to fall. Her hands are in her lap and the tears fall onto her hands and wet her skirt.

No matter what, I love my mom. And at this moment, I don't care about anything else but my mom's tears and my need to make them stop. I sit up, wrap my arms around my mom, and hug her tight. She opens up her arms and hugs me back, just as tight. This is the first time in a long time that I can remember hugging and being hugged by my mom. We aren't touchy-feely. But this time, it feels so good. Somehow, we both know we need a hug.

We lean back and look at each other through our tears, since I have started crying again too. We laugh through our tears, and Mom says, "I must look a mess."

"Join the crowd," I say. We both laugh again. Mom drops her arms and grabs my hand. She looks into my eyes again.

"I am sorry, Daijha, for how things have been between us."
She sighs. "I have been selfish, but I promise it will get better.
We are going to make it through this."

I can't speak 'cause I'm afraid I'll start crying again, so
I just nod. She drops my hand and heads to the bathroom. I
lie back on my bed and look up at the ceiling. It has been a
crazy week.

Mom pops her head back around my door. "I called Doris.
I let her know we wouldn't be coming today."

Though I want to go to church, I am relieved to not be
going today.

"Okay, Mom. Was she disappointed?"

"Probably a little, but when I explained to her a little about
what happened between us just now, she understood."

"What?" I sit up. Mom never tells people "family business."
She would probably smack me upside my head if she knew I
ever told anyone some of our "family business"!

"What made you tell her that?"

Mom stands quietly, thinking for a second.

"You know, when I was over there the other day, she prayed
for me in the kitchen. At first I was uncomfortable—I mean,
she asked if she could pray for us, but who does that?" She
shrugs her shoulders.

"But I said okay and she prayed. She calls me every day
to check on me. It's kinda nice." She smiled. "So it kinda
just came out when we were talking just now, and she said
another prayer."

Mom looks at me. "Close your mouth, Daijha."

I close my mouth, but I am still looking at my mom in shock.

She laughs and shakes her head. "Change your clothes. We're about to leave."

She leaves my room and goes to hers. I learned a long time ago not to ask where we were going, 'cause when you asked, you were subject to getting left at home. And the truth is that it doesn't really matter. As long as we are getting out of the house, I am game.

Chapter 8

Pulling the car away from the curb, Mom turns to me and asks, "You ready for a day of fun?"

"Heck yeah!" I know my smile shows every tooth I have in my head, but I don't care. I am excited!

First we drive over to my dad's. Mom tells me to stay in the car while she goes in the house. She and my dad come out a few minutes later, and my dad's face breaks into a smile when he sees me in the car. He comes to the window.

"Hey, baby girl! Happy birthday—again!" He already called this morning to tell me happy birthday.

"Thanks, Dad." I smile and get out of the car to give him a hug. Dad wraps me up in his arms and swings me around. I giggle and hug him tight.

He puts me down. "I'll see you later on tonight. And stop looking around for a gift!" Dad says when he catches me looking over his shoulder at the porch.

"Have a good time with your mom today, okay?"

"Okay, Dad." Mom and I get back into the car, and we are on our way.

Mom pulls up to a popular teen clothing store. She turns and looks at me.

"Your dad gave me some money he saved for your birthday, and I have some money I saved for it too. Maurice also sent me some money for you today. I don't want you to worry about anything today but having a good time, okay?"

I frown a little. I get Mom's meaning, but I can't help but think about the possibility of her losing her job.

"Are you sure, Mom? We could—"

"Daijha." She has that warning tone in her voice.

I hold up my hands in surrender. "Okay, Mom."

I can't help it. I begin to smile really big and can barely keep my self from flinging the door open and running toward the store. I know we could—and probably should—save the money for bills or something, but I am so happy to be able to spend it on me!

"You have $275 to spend on clothes and shoes." My mouth drops open.

"You serious, Mom? Two hundred and seventy-five? For me?"

"Yes. You have to get some dress clothes and dress shoes, but after that—"

"Yes!" I scream after I throw open my car door and jump out. I jog toward my mom's door to meet her as she gets out of the car. I bounce from one foot to the other.

Mom looks at me and laughs. "Girl, you are like a puppy!"

She laughs again and we head toward the store. A few people turn to look at me, and, suddenly embarrassed, I quiet down.

I fall into step with my mom. This was quickly becoming one of the best days of my life!

*****

Mom and I spend the day shopping. We go from store to store and find some really good sales. I am able to find two skirts, two tops, a dress, and a pair of black dress shoes, all for church. The skirts are both denim. One is simple and stops just above my knees, and the other falls just below my knees, ends in lace, and has ice-blue stitching. I got a black button-down shirt to go with the simple skirt and an ice-blue V-neck sweater to match the stitching on the other.

The dress is a simple black jersey one to replace my old one. All of that cost about seventy-five dollars.

With the remaining money, we buy a hot pair of name-brand gym shoes—on sale! They aren't the latest shoes, but I don't care. We also find a pair of boots that all the girls are wearing, three pairs of jeans, a pair of cargo khakis, and four tops. One shirt has a red lacy design on the front, one is a hot pink polo, one is a tan sweater/shirt that looks like a sweater over a white button-down, and a scarlet and gray college hoodie. We also buy some new underwear and socks.

It is late in the afternoon, and mom and I have really enjoyed our time together. She has a pretty good sense of style and helped me piece my clothes together.

"Thanks, Mom, for today! This has been the best day ever. I can't wait to see J and show her all my new things. I can't wait to go to school tomorrow!" I smile at her and then turn to look out the window.

Mom reaches over and squeezes my knee, smiles, and says, "You're welcome, but the day isn't over yet."

She pulls into the parking lot of my favorite restaurant.

"We still have money for dinner?" I look at Mom. I thought we spent all the money, if not more than that.

"Hush, girl, and come on."

We walk into the restaurant and the hostess greets us.

"Just the two of you?"

Mom nods yes. The hostess grabs two menus. "Right this way."

We fall in line behind the hostess, and as we turn the corner, I hear "Surprise!" and a boatload of people begin to sing "Happy Birthday."

I am so shocked. I look around at all the people: Jazmyn, her youth group, her mom and little sisters, my dad, my brother and his wife, and my sister, niece, nephew, and her new husband.

I smile, and for the second time in the same day, I am sure all of the teeth in my head are showing. But I don't care at all!

Everyone sits down after they finish the song and clap, as do many other people in the restaurant, and I see, on the table behind them, several presents.

Ms. D sees me looking at the gifts in surprise and says, "We couldn't resist, Daijha! When we found out it was your birthday today, we asked your mom if we could share it with you and your family. So here we are!" She spreads her arms to encompass everyone and laughs, and so does everyone else.

"Thanks" doesn't seem like enough, so I walk over to her and quickly give her a hug and thank her.

She smiles real big and hugs me back. "You're welcome."

Mom steps over and gives her a hug too. We all sit down to dinner and have a fantastic time. I open my presents after we all finish eating. Everyone in the youth group chipped in and bought me a youth study Bible and a journal to write in. Jazmyn and her mom bought me a nice set of drawing pencils and some sketch paper. (Jazmyn said she saw some of my work on the wall at school and could see how much I liked to draw with pencil.)

At the end of the evening, Maurice says he has an announcement. He stands up.

"Daijha, I am so glad to be here to share in your birthday. And since we are all here, there is no better time to share our news."

He looks down at his wife with a big ol' smile. "Christina is pregnant!"

Everyone yells and claps, especially Mom, Reeni, and me. Maurice and Christina have been trying to get pregnant for a couple years, and Christina has miscarried a couple times. I take a better look at Christina, and her stomach is noticeably swollen. I am not the only one thinking this.

Reeni laughs and says, "Girl, I thought you were looking a little fluffy ... but I knew better than to ask! Congratulations! How far along are you?"

Christina blushes. "Fluffy?!"

Reeni laughs and Christina joins in. "We're three months."

"What?" Reeni, Mom, Ms. D, and I say at once.

Maurice, now sitting down, puts his arm around Christina protectively.

"We wanted to be sure this time." He looks at Mom. "We just didn't want to get our—or anyone else's—hopes up until we knew she would carry this one to term."

We are all so excited. The conversation turns toward plans for the baby. I just sit back and watch. This is the happiest I have been in a long time.

Chapter 9

"So you and your mom are definitely coming to church this Sunday?" Jazmyn asks me on our way to school.

I laugh. "Yes!"

It has been two weeks since my birthday, but my mom and I haven't been able to make it to church yet. Last weekend, my mom surprised me when she took me to get micro braids. Christina talked to a friend of hers who does hair, and I was able to get my hair done. Maurice told my mom not to worry about it and paid for it.

I wonder why so many good things are happening in my life lately. I am kind of used to being let down. I even asked Reeni why Maurice was being so nice. He and I have never really been close. Even before he moved out, he was doing his own thing—sports, girls, work. I was surprised that he would just offer to get my hair done.

Reeni said that he really didn't know what was going on when he left. He said he would have helped Mom more, but she never told him about her problems. I asked why she didn't have any problem asking Reeni for money, but not Maurice. Reeni said she didn't know and to stop asking so many questions and just be thankful! I laughed after that and stopped asking questions.

"Good," Jazmym said, bringing me back to the present. "I am excited for you to come!"

"Me too."

Jazmyn and I have become really good friends. We spend time together at her house almost every day after school. Her mom and my mom are getting along pretty well and talk on the phone often. Some days, my mom will come pick me up when she gets off work, and she'll come in and talk to Ms. D. Other days, she'll just call, and I'll walk home—if it isn't dark yet.

After homeroom and the bell, Jazmyn and I walk to class. We take our seats, and I happen to catch Jerome's eye. He and Natasha are talking, but her back is to me. He looks at me and just looks back to Natasha—no comments, no nothing.

I smile to myself. I'm starting to get used to this. Ever since Jazmyn stood up to him, Jerome has left us alone. My new clothes and hair are just icing on the cake. And since Jerome leaves us alone, Natasha leaves us alone—though Natasha took a little more convincing.

Last week, she and a couple of her girls came into the bathroom when Jazmyn and I were in there. "Look at the beached whale and her dirty sidekick!" Natasha hollered, and her girls started laughing. I looked at Jazmyn and she closed her eyes real quick before turning to Natasha.

"What is your problem, Natasha? I have done nothing to you, nor has Daijha. Grow up already and stop being so hateful. I'm not afraid of you or your words. I look at me in the mirror every day, and I love me. But if tearing me down makes you feel as if you are better than me, so be it. I know the truth."

Natasha frowned and opened her mouth to say something, but J and I brushed past her and walked out of the bathroom. I glanced back at Natasha. She rolled her eyes and turned to the mirror.

I've noticed that she and Jerome feed off others' feelings of insecurity or what they think is weakness. If you don't show them either one, they have nothing to feed off of.

This was another time I was in awe of Jazmyn, but she reminded me that it wasn't about her, but Who was in her.

Thinking back to this, I can't wait to get to her church on Sunday and see what this is all about. I want to feel that strength and power on the inside.

Chapter 10

I smile at myself in the mirror. This Sunday morning is way different from the Sunday a couple weeks back. I have on the new black dress and black dress shoes I got on my birthday. My hair is pulled back in a loose ponytail with a few braids framing my face. I am finally beginning to believe that I am kind of pretty—well, at least that I don't blind anyone!

"Daijha, you ready?" Mom peeks into the bathroom.

"Wow, lady, don't you look nice!"

I smile. "Thanks, Mom. Yes, I'm ready."

I turn and follow Mom out of the bathroom. "You don't look too shabby yourself, Ma."

She has on a long denim skirt, a brown button-down shirt, and a pair of brown mules.

"Why, thank you," Mom says on our way down the stairs. We are going to head over to Jazmyn's and follow her family to church.

*****

"Praise the Lord, church!"

The man on the piano, who is leading the choir, shouts to congregation.

"Praise the Lord!" the church responds enthusiastically.

Mom and I sit with Jazmyn and her family in a pew near the middle of the church. When we came in, there were quite a few people already here, and after about three songs, the church is almost full. During the praise and worship, people are standing and singing along.

Though there is praise and worship at my dad's church, it is nothing like this! The music is so strong, and there is a feeling of excitement and expectation that I can't explain. I feel all warm and good inside. I even sing along with a few songs, reading the lyrics off the screens mounted on the front walls.

After another couple of songs, the man at the piano motions for us to sit down, so we do.

Pastor Avermond (Jazmyn told me his name) walks to the front and asks if there are any first-time visitors. Mom and I stand up, along with a few other people scattered throughout the church.

The visitors take turns introducing themselves, and when it is our turn, Mom speaks for us.

"Hello. My name is Janet, and this is my daughter Daijha. We are friends of Doris and Jazmyn, who invited us."

People smile and clap. Pastor Avermond tells us all that he is thankful that we came to visit and that if we need a church home, we could join this one. He then announces that it is time for fellowship, and most everyone gets up and walks around, greeting each other with hugs and blessings. So many people come over and shake our hands and hug us that I lose count.

After about five or ten minutes, the pastor calls us all back to our seats, and the choir sings a couple more songs. At the end of the second song, the pastor walks to the pulpit and asks us to grab our Bibles and stand. As people stand up, he dismisses all the kids who are participating in youth and children's church.

Before we came, Jazmyn told me that youth and children's church was for all the kids, visitors and members alike, from ages three to eighteen, and that at youth and children's church, the children are broken up into groups by age. Her group is ten- to fourteen-year-olds.

"So how do you like it so far, Daijha?" Jazmyn asks me as we walk down the stairs to class.

"I like it, J. The music was nice and the people are so friendly."

"Yeah, we're a friendly bunch." J smiles. "You sure get your hugs for the week!"

I laugh. "I know that's right!"

When we get downstairs, Jazmyn leads me to her group's room. I look around at the posters and artwork on the walls about all sorts of topics—the Ten Commandments, encouraging quotes, and messages about looking out for one another.

The room is clean and bright with three round tables with seven chairs at each. We spot Andre and Marie at one table and join them. Another girl I recognize as a visitor sits down with us.

When the teacher, a young lady with caramel skin and a baby Afro and dressed in a black skirt and pink button-down top, enters, she sees that there are two tables with four kids and one with five. She asks one table with four to split up and join one of the other two tables. She passes out worksheets and introduces herself as Sister Mary.

"Okay, everyone. Take a pen out of the middle container and answer the questions on your paper."

I look down and see that the questions are about peer pressure. I am confused and wonder what peer pressure has to do with church. I look over at Jazmyn and see that she is busy following Sister Mary's instructions. She isn't the least bit confused, so I shrug my shoulders and begin to answer mine.

After a few minutes, Sister Mary asks us to put our pens down. She points to Andre.

"Okay, Andre, so what is peer pressure?"

"Um … it's like when kids try to get you to do something."

"Yes, it is. Does anyone else have anything they want to add?"

One girl raises her hand.

Sister Mary nods and asks, "What's your name?"

"Jada."

Sister Mary smiles. "Okay, Jada, what do you think?"

"Peer pressure is usually when your friends try to talk you into doing or saying something that you don't want to do or say."

"Thanks, Jada, for adding a little more to it. And Jada, is peer pressure always negative?"

Jada pauses. I wonder how peer pressure could be good. It's never a good thing to try and make someone do something they don't want to do. Jazmyn raises her hand.

"Yes, Jazmyn?"

"No, Sister Mary, sometimes peer pressure can be positive."

I see Andre nodding his head in agreement, but a few other kids, like me, are a little confused.

Sister Mary smiles and nods. "Explain, Jazmyn."

"Well, sometimes friends might try to get you to smoke or drink or have sex. These are all negative. But sometimes, friends might try to get you try something new and exciting, like getting on a roller coaster or trying some new foods. Or they can try to get you to come to church with them. These are examples of positive peer pressure."

"You're exactly right, Jazmyn! Sometimes, friends can try to get you to do something that is not right, and other times, they can try to get you to do some things that are good. We are talking about this today because negative peer pressure is serious. And succumbing to it, or giving in, can lead to some serious consequences. You can find yourself in a whole lot of trouble that won't be easy to get out of if you make some decisions based on what your friends want you to do. The first issue that you need to be aware of is the types of friends that you have."

Sister Mary walks over to the board and writes "Proverbs 13:20."

Everyone grabs a Bible from the piles in the middle of the tables. Sister Mary waits a minute for everyone to find the verse and reads it.

"The Bible says in Proverbs 13:20 of the King James Version, 'He that walketh with wise men shall be wise: but a companion of fools shall be destroyed.' What do you think that means?"

Marie raises her hand.

Sister Mary nods. "Go ahead, Marie."

"Well, I think it means if you hang around people who are smart and are doing what's right, then you'll end up doing what's right and being smart too. But if you hang around people who aren't about nothing, then they'll end up getting you to act like them."

"That's right, Marie. Basically, you are who you hang with. And foolish people—they find trouble! If you are a good person who is doing what you are supposed to do and spend time with people who might be good people too but are making bad choices and aren't concerned with doing right—they'll rub off on you. You won't rub off on them!"

"But I thought we were supposed to be a light in the darkness ... in the world, like it says in Matthew 5:14, and show others the right way," Adam says. He and a few others came in a few minutes late and are sitting at another table.

"Well, yes, Adam, we are supposed to shine our light by living right and allowing others to see that. But when it comes to picking people for those special spaces in your life reserved for friendship, you must choose wisely.

"Again, Proverbs 13:20 says, 'He that walketh with wise men shall be wise: but a companion of fools shall be destroyed.' The 'walking' part is key. That means living your daily life with someone."

For the next hour, we talk more about how to avoid negative peer pressure, including listening to your parents. Sister Mary tells us to read Ephesians 6:1-3 and to follow it regarding our choice of friends and behavior and to not allow ourselves to get into situations where we can be negatively pressured.

We also talk about not waiting for people to find you but instead joining groups that will have a positive influence on our physical, emotional, and spiritual development.

Near the end of Sunday school, we have a snack and free time.

Jazmyn gets up and talks to a couple of kids, but I just sit there. I have a lot on my mind. I never thought the Bible really related to me—like, I know there is stuff in there telling me how to live, like don't kill or steal, but peer pressure? I am suddenly filled with a strong urge to know more. I open the Bible to Proverbs again and begin to flip through.

Jazmyn interrupts my thoughts. "You all right?"

"Yeah." I glance up at J but return my gaze to the words in front of me. I know what the words mean, but I don't quite know what they mean to me.

J's words cut through my thoughts again. "Looks like you have a lot on your mind."

I nod. I want to know more about the Bible and what it says about my life. I want to know how to be confident in who I am, like Jazmyn and the rest of the kids in youth group. I want to know "Whose" I am. And even though I can't quite understand the words' meaning for me now, I know, deep inside, that these answers are in the Bible.

"Well, you can talk to me about anything ... or my mom," Jazmyn offers.

I nod. "I know. Thanks, girl."

"No prob. You ready to go back up?"

I look around and notice the others gathering their things, so I gather mine and follow J out the door. When we get back upstairs, the pastor is finishing altar call. This is the time when people can come up to give their lives to Christ and be saved, join the church, and/or have a special prayer.

I see my mom up front and stop in my tracks and stare. Andre is behind me and nudges me forward. I gather myself and continue to follow Jazmyn to our seats. Her mom is in front with my mom and tears are running down both of their faces. They are facing us, and the pastor is standing off to the right. A lady I do not know introduces my mom. "Church, this is Janet Compton. She has decided to rededicate her life to God and make this her church home!"

Everyone starts clapping and shouting. I am so overwhelmed that I start to cry. I have seen people dedicate their lives to Christ, and I have seen people accept salvation, but it has never really been my desire. I believe in God, but I guess I always thought that salvation was for adulthood.

The pastor holds up his hand and everyone starts to quiet down.

"I know I don't normally do this, but before I tell Janet that this is the best decision she has ever made and what an honor it is for her to join our church, I'm being led to ask—is there someone else here who knows they need to give their life to God and accept Jesus Christ as their Lord and Savior?"

Before I can stop myself, I step out into the aisle. My mom and I lock eyes through our tears. I take a deep breath and walk down the aisle to join my mom and accept salvation.

Adolescence can be an awful experience for children. Children who are outcasts, for whatever reason, often find themselves isolated and alone, hoping that someone will take the chance to get to know them but too afraid to reach out themselves.

However, this experience doesn't have to be awful. If we can step outside our fears and extend friendship to someone who may not be just like us, we can cut down on the Daijhas, children who feel alone, isolated, and friendless, and increase the Jazmyns, children bold enough to reach out to others and stand up for themselves in the process.

C. Angel grew up in Ohio and currently resides in a suburb of Columbus with her three children and puppy. Books have always been a form of immense enjoyment and escape for her, from picking a corner and reading for hours as a young child in a library to curling up on the couch with a book and a nice blanket as an adult. She is a licensed history teacher by trade and an author by choice. *Daijha Road* is her first published work.